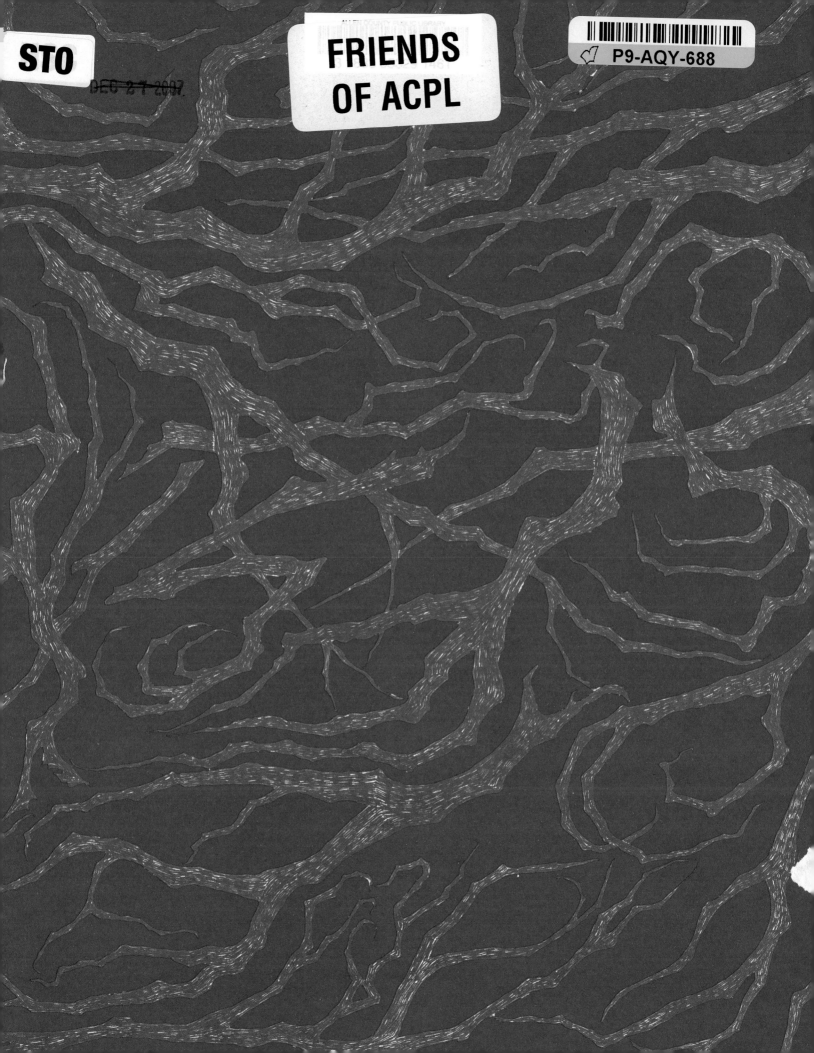

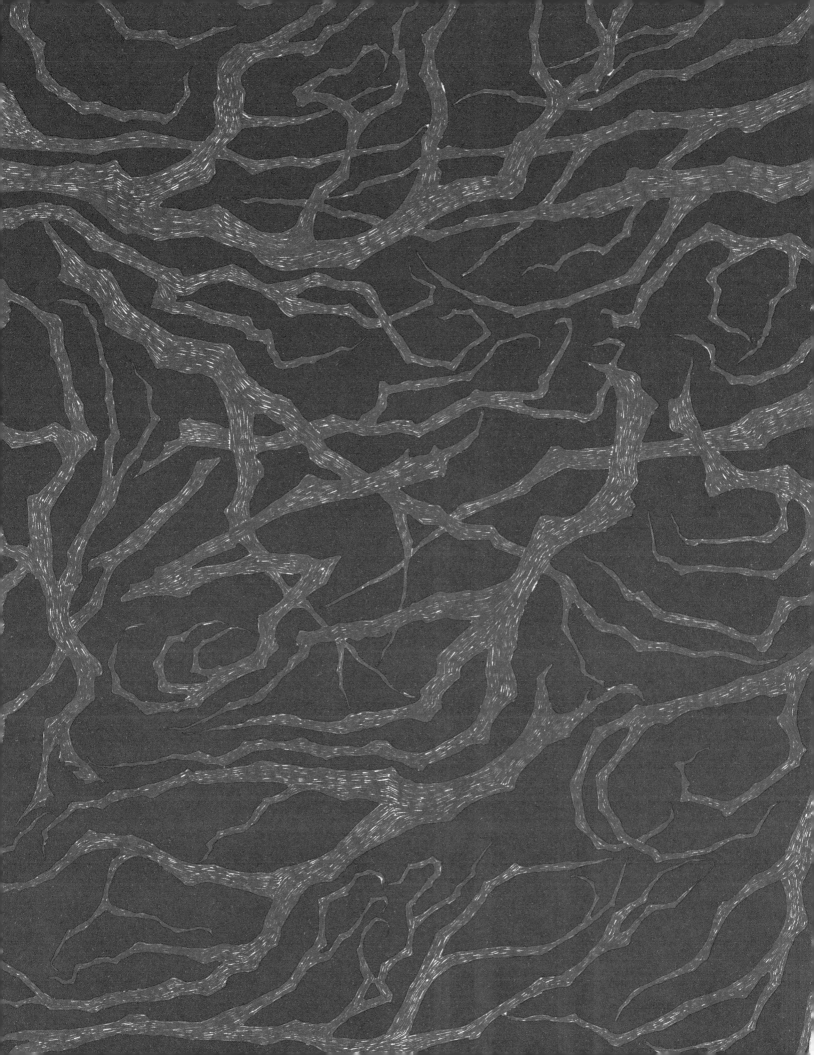

The Ürl King

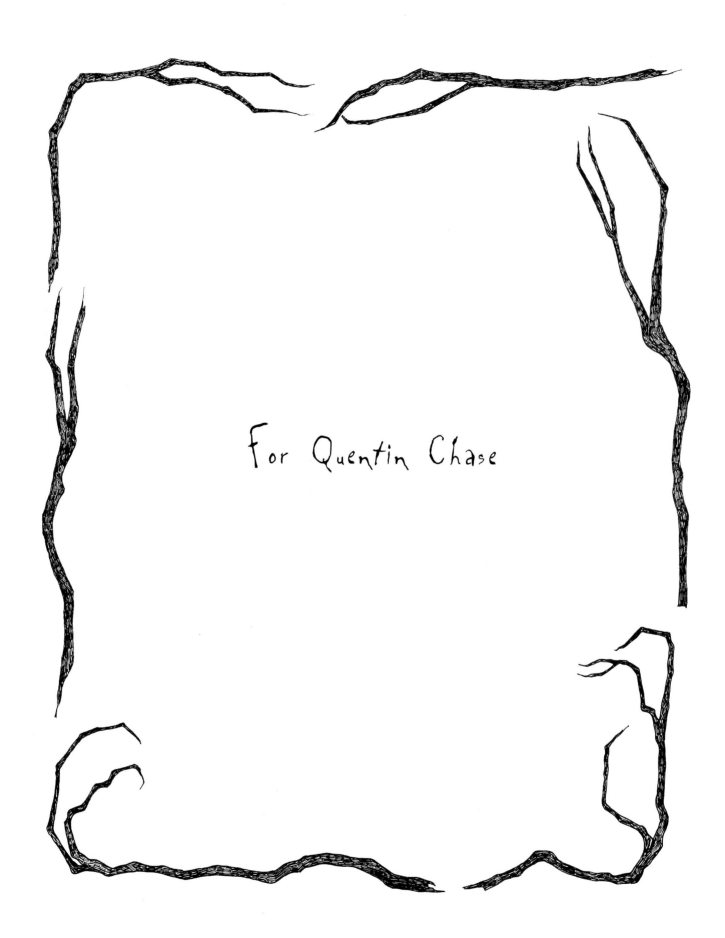

For Quentin Chase

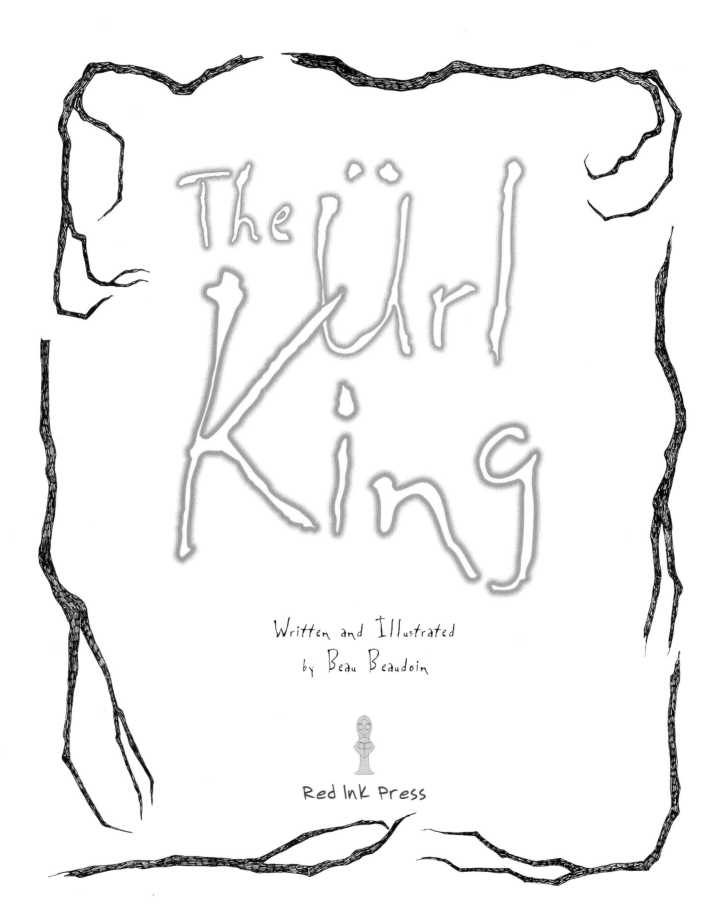

The Ürl King

Written and Illustrated
by Beau Beaudoin

Red Ink Press

This is Jeremiah, Jeremiah La'Sort.
His dog ran into the woods,
So he called out for Bucksnort.
"Here Bucksnort! Here boy!"
He listened real quietly for Bucksnort's bark.
The boy was quite scared, for it was starting to get dark.

"Come here boy. You know what we were told.

We are not allowed in these woods;

it's spooky and cold."

The boy called out again, "Here Bucksnort!"

Then, from behind him came a sound.

Jeremiah La'Sort slowly turned around.

It's not for certain what Jeremiah had seen

That caused his eyes to widen and him to let out the most horrible scream.

Many in town must have heard Jeremiah's scream,

shortly thereafter...

The police were at the scene.

They could not imagine what Jeremiah had seen that night.

They found him scared stiff, eyes wide and his hair turned white.

One officer said,

"I wonder what it was that could cause this sort of fear?"

Another officer replied,

"I don't know, but it's the fifth one this year."

There is something in all of us,

Whether in daytime or in dreams,

Which causes one goose bumps, shivers or screams.

Fear is a part of everyone, causing one to be nervous or scared,

except for one boy who is frightened impaired.

This is the story of Simon, a boy much different than most.

Simon cannot be scared, not by monsters, spiders or even ghosts.

Sure, the children and teachers think he is weird,

however, they criticize Simon

to cover up all the silly things they have feared.

Simon wants to know fear.

He has searched for it week after week.

Not being like others makes him feel like a freak.

Simon has read many scary books

and seen all the horror movies one could see,

And stays up late at night to watch monster movies on TV.

He has been to haunted houses...

and the
creepiest graveyard.
Simon doesn't understand
why getting scared is so hard.

He had almost given up until that day on the playground,

When he heard the children talking about Jeremiah La'Sort being found.

The children gathered around telling the stories that they heard,

Of what frightened that boy, Simon listened closely to every word.

"My Uncle said it's aliens that have come from outer space."

"It's probably a witch. You know they're all over the place."

"I bet it's a monster," one boy said.

"Maybe even the monster that's under my bed."

"What ever it is must be really scary.

It probably has fangs and claws."

"I wonder if it's slimy or hairy?"

Then one boy spoke out.

"Don't be silly. We all know it could be just one thing.

It's the most dreadful of all..."

One girl cried out "you don't mean..."

"Yes! The Ürl King!"

The children all muttered and made sounds of fear.

This was a subject Simon wanted to hear.

Simon asked the boy, "What's the Ürl King?

What can he do?"

The boy answered,

"He can scare the life out of anyone.

Even a freak like you."

Simon thought to himself, is it possible, could this be?

Can the Ürl King put some fear into me?

Simon didn't hesitate. He didn't think twice.

He ran to the house of the man

who just so happened to look a little like Vincent Price.

In hope that he might possess some information he wants to know.

Perhaps the man can show him the correct way to go.

"Foolish boy," responded the man.

"Do you know what you ask?"

"This is no person in a silly mask.

But the Ürl King!

Feared by all and not most.

He is not simply an illusion or a ghost."

"Simon, I understand to be scared is your goal.

However, the Ürl King desires more than simply to scare you.

The Ürl King wants your soul!"

Simon responded,

"This all sounds so great. What more can I say?

I shall meet this Ürl King on this very day!

But how shall I find him?

Is he a person, creature or thing?

Please sir, explain to me. What is the Ürl King?"

Reaching to the mantle the man picked up a book...

then, as he sat down he gave Simon a distressed look.

Who rides so late throughout the dark of the night?

In the woods when the wind is so wild.

On a horse ride a father and his young child.

He holds the boy within his arm.

He clasps him tightly, to keep him warm.

"My son why do you hide your face in fear?"

"See father, the Ürl King is near.

The Ürl King with its crown and shroud."

"My son, it's only a misty cloud."

"You lovely child, come, go with me.

Such pleasant games I shall play with thee.

Beyond these woods are flowers bright to behold.

I shall warm you up with robes of gold."

"My father, my father, now don't you hear,

What the Ürl King whispers in my ear?"

"Be calm, be calm and still my child.

The dry leaves rustle when the wind blows wild.

My lovely boy, won't you go with me?

My daughters all shall wait on thee."

"My daughter's youth shall always keep.

They shall sing, dance and rock thee to sleep."

"My Father, my Father, can't you see the face,

Of the Ürl King's daughters in that dark place?"

"My son, my son, all I can see

is just that old gray willow tree."

"Father! Father! He's grabbing my arm!

The Ürl King wishes to do me great harm!"

The father shuddered. He sped through the cold.

He looked down at his son and tightened his hold.

What the boy was encountering the father couldn't tell.

But knew something was terribly wrong when he

heard his son yell.

The father reached home with pain and dread.

The boy lay in his arms appearing to be dead.

But he wasn't, he was scared stiff

and his hair had turned white.

The Ürl King took his soul from fear that night.

"So did this story I read to you help you contemplate?

Did it cause you to change your mind?"

"Are you kidding?" asked Simon.

"This all sounds so great!

But what if this Ürl King cannot show me fear?

Surely he must with all that I hear."

"That I don't know.

Perhaps all his powers would be gone.

I suppose without a soul he cannot go on."

Simon headed for the door as fast as he could.

The man told him to be careful.

Simon told him he would.

Simon entered the woods hoping he would leave knowing fear.

He walked through the woods calling out,

"Okay Ürl King. I am here."

He walked for a while and was real pleased to see

That standing before him was an old gray willow tree.

Simon thought to himself

I'll hang out here and have me a look,

Surely this is the tree that was mentioned in the book.

Simon waited for a while and was getting disappointed and tired.

So, he sat on a log.

Then, came creeping through the woods was a thickening fog.

Simon saw amongst the fog, surrounding the tree

Was a young girl standing there?

At first there was one, then there were two girls and then three.

With a melancholy look they simply stood there.

They had dark, empty eyes and raven black hair.

The fog got thicker. The woods suddenly got dark.

Then, from behind him came a sound. It sounded like a bark.

The winds picked up, the cold gave Simon a chill.

Then, out came a dog, with three legs and a wheel.

He knew this dog. It belonged to Jeremiah La'Sort.

Now what is his name he thought? Oh yes, his name is Bucksnort.

Suddenly, from a distance beyond the tree

Came a light brighter than fire.

Bucksnort took off running as fast as he could,

But the poor dog had a flat tire.

Simon called out to the dog....

"Don't leave Bucksnort, don't run through the wood.

Stay here with me. This is finally getting good."

Then, he heard a voice, whisper among the wind.

"My boy, why aren't you running with your dog scared?"

"Well, you see I have a problem." Simon replied.

"I am frightened impaired.

I am here for you to scare me. That is my goal."

"Oh, I'll scare you... And then I'll take your soul."

Simon added, "Don't get your hopes up. We'll just have to see.

So give me your worst, please, don't be humoring me."

Simon got ready, he rolled up his sleeves.

Suddenly, something stirred from under the leaves.

A skeleton arose! Then, to add to the surprise,

A snake crawled of its mouth and back into its eyes.

Simon looked at the skeleton and asked with a grin:

"How are you this evening? You're looking quite thin."

Simon rolled his sleeves back down.

The evening's air was starting to get colder.

The skeleton approached Simon and reached out to his shoulder.

Simon didn't say a word, he didn't make a sound.

The skeleton's bones fell a part and tumbled on the ground.

Simon tried to call the Ürl King's bluff and said...

"Well, its looks like I'll be the winner.

I should probably get going so I won't be late for dinner."

Suddenly, the trees came alive and let out howls and screams.

Simon didn't even flinch, he had seen worse in his dreams.

Then the leaves came up from the ground and

Shaped into ghouls that cried out a great yell.

Simon was quite impressed, but then sneezed and
All the leaves fell.
"Well thanks for trying and thanks for the show.
But I really think that perhaps I should go.
That trick with the leaves was really great.
I would like to see more.
However, it's getting quite late.
So try once more.
What else is up your sleeve?
This is your last chance.
I am going to leave."

Then coming from behind him he heard a sound.

Not knowing what to expect, Simon slowly turned around.

What Simon had seen caught him by surprise.

He dropped his mouth open and widened his eyes.

It must have been quite amazing what Simon had seen that night.

It caused a piece of his hair to turn white.

Simon said, "Wow! That's the scariest thing I've ever seen! That certainly made this night worth staying out. Even if it is nine sixteen."

Simon had seen the Ürl King's worst and still no fear.

Simon then watched the Ürl King disappear.

Later, Simon came out of the woods accompanied by
The three legged dog Bucksnort.
Standing there were the townsfolk, and five thankful children.
Including Jeremiah La'Sort.
A police officer said,
"Simon, whatever you did you did very well.
All of the children are out of their spell."

One girl asked, "Simon, how many times did you get scared?"

Simon answered in a disappointed voice, "Zero."

The girl responded,

"Your being different from others has made you a hero!"

Simon headed home and though he didn't experience
any shivers from fright,
He couldn't help but crack a smile, all in all,
It was a pretty fun night.

The End

Acknowledgements

With thanks to:
Johann Wolfgang Von Goethe, Vincent Price,
Hayden Foell, George McAtee, Sreed, Beth Wright
and especially... Sarah.

Red Ink Press
www.redinkpress.com
Text and Illustations © 2006 by Beau Beaudoin Publishing, Inc

Designed by Hayden Foell & Iain Morris

Printed in China by Palace Press International

Library of Congress Cataloguing-In-Publication Data
The Url King / Beau Beaudoin - 1st ed.
p. cm.
Summary: A boy who has never feared anything
ventures into the woods
to seek out a legend said to be the scariest of all things.
ISBN 0-9788401-0-0
Stories in rhyme 1.Title
LCCN- 2006907685

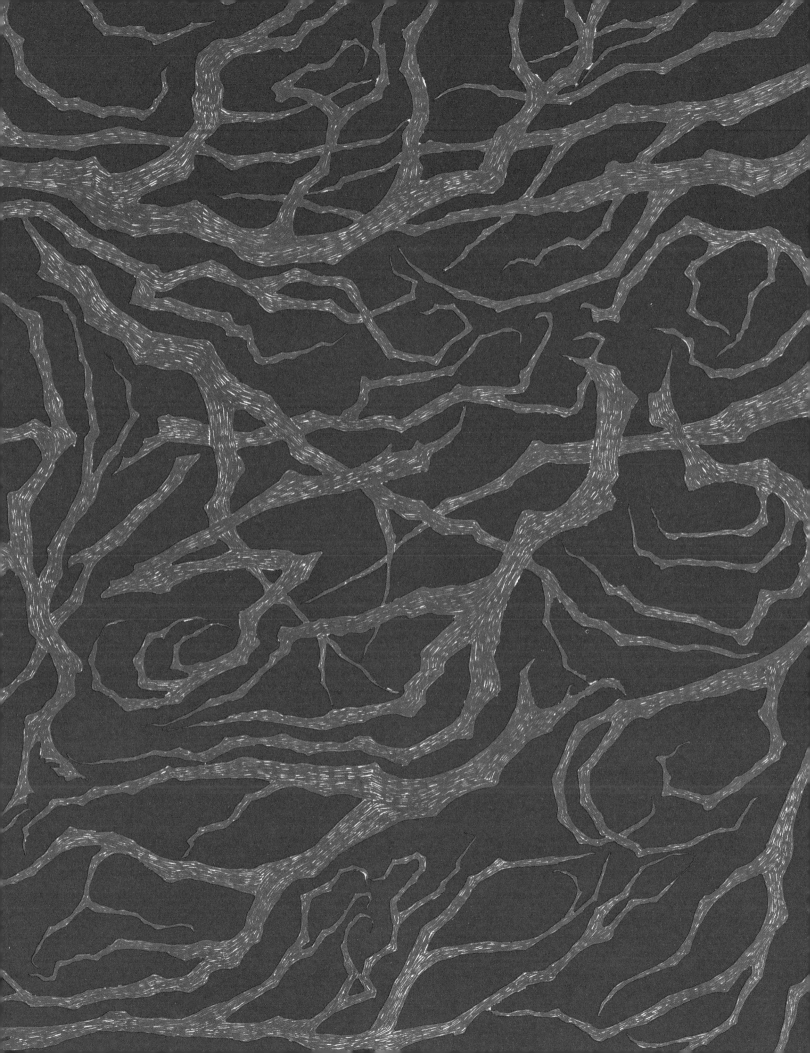